Are YOU a Valoraptor?

Christine Davies

Grosvenor House
Publishing Limited

The right of Christine Davies to be identified as the author of this
work has been asserted in accordance with Section 78
of the Copyright, Designs and Patents Act 1988

The book cover is copyright to Christine Davies

This book is published by
Grosvenor House Publishing Ltd
Link House
140 The Broadway, Tolworth, Surrey, KT6 7HT.
www.grosvenorhousepublishing.co.uk

A CIP record for this book
is available from the British Library

ISBN 978-1-83975-875-1

Are You a Valoraptor?

Brave little Valo hatches from his egg and finds himself all alone in the world.

Who is he?

Where are his mummy and daddy?

How does he find others of his own kind?

Join Valo and his dinosaur friends on his journey through this ancient landscape to try to find his family.

This little book is written for my precious, funny, beautiful grandson Valo who blesses our lives every day. It is wonderful watching you grow and I can't wait to see what the future holds for you.

Also, to Russell and Claire, and Amber her family and to Nigel & Squire!.

Special thanks to the lovely Lily Willow Holdsworth for her wonderful illustrations which capture the personalities of the little characters and bring them to life in a very special way.

I hope you enjoy travelling with Valo on his adventures.

iii

Are YOU a Valoraptor?

Valo's story begins when he was very small. So small in fact that he lived inside a very special egg which his mummy and daddy took great care to keep warm and safe. The egg was a beautiful cream colour with pretty purple markings, but Valo didn't know that. His whole world was INSIDE the egg where it was cosy, snug and dark. Curled up and comfy, Valo could often hear his parents talking on the outside, and even his mother singing to him. Sometimes, he wondered what the world was like outside of his egg, but mostly, he just slept and continued to grow.

His parents had built a wonderful nest in a scraped out hollow near to the base of a tall cliff. The nest was lined with small twigs, grass and leaves, and around the edge, his father had laid a ring of small white stones to mark the boundary. Each stone had been carefully chosen and the result was stunning. The area around their home was mainly grass and desert, but there was a small stream nearby to provide

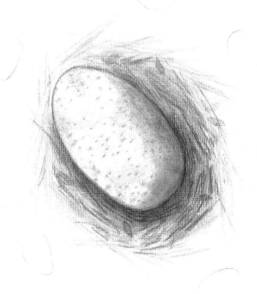

water and where they could catch fish to eat. They were so looking forward to the day when their baby would break out of the egg and join them.

One day, the two adults decided to venture a little farther from the nest to go in search of food. The nest was well hidden and they were sure that their precious egg would be safe for a short while.

"Goodbye little one" his mother whispered, "we won't be long"

With that, the two grownups scampered off. It was very quiet in the egg, and Valo was dreaming about what he might see and do when it was time for him to leave the egg. It was very hard for him to imagine what the outside world might be like, what the sights and smells might be, and he tried to imagine what everything would be like. After a while though, he drifted off to sleep again.

Suddenly he heard a loud screaming cawing noise which startled him awake. What ever could it be? The noises were nothing like his parent's voices, and Valo was quite frightened. Then, he felt the egg start to roll around! He began to be feel quite dizzy – what was happening? He could hear a scraping noise on the outside of the shell and the screaming was getting louder and angrier. Just then Valo heard a shout and recognised his mother's voice, but then a very strange and scary thing happened. He felt his egg (with him inside) lift off the ground and up into the air. He could hear the shouts of his parents but their voices were growing fainter until he could no longer hear them.

Poor little dinosaur. His nest had been spotted by two huge pterodactyls who had spied the egg and decided to break it open. Despite rolling the egg around, the shell had been too strong and before they could try something else to break it, his parents had arrived back at the nest. They rushed towards the raptors, but the flying reptiles had seen them, and one of them had grabbed the egg in its claws and flown up into the sky. The two adults couldn't reach the egg in time, and could only watch in horror as the raptors carried the egg and their baby up into the sky and flew away over the top of the cliff.

Inside the egg, the poor baby was feeling terrified. Even though there was not much room inside the egg, he was rolling around inside the shell and bouncing up and down as the huge creature carried him away from his nest. Never having seen the outside world, he had no idea what was happening, but he knew he didn't like the feeling and just wanted to be safely back home with his parents. The pterodactyls flew on and on, over the grassland and trees and across a small river. They were heading back to a huge tree where they had built their nest high up on the top most branches.

CAAAWWW! Another loud scream and Valo felt his captor plunge down and to one side. The pterodactyl was being attacked by another raptor who was determined to steal the egg! The movements became faster and jerkier until without warning Valo felt himself falling through the air. The raptor has dropped the egg! Faster and faster he fell, with no way to stop.

CRASH! He landed with a huge thump on the ground. The egg rolled a short distance and then stopped. Valo had closed his eyes tightly as he fell, but now he opened them. To his shock he could see a bright light coming through a large crack in the shell. What should he do? He couldn't stay in the egg, but he was afraid to move and try to break out of it. Usually, his parents would be there to greet and support him as he emerged, but he was all alone and still in danger. Above him, he could hear the flying creatures screaming at each other, and somehow, he just knew that he had to be brave and try to get away from the noise and the danger.

Wriggling around, he pushed his feet against the crack in the shell and pushed as hard as he could. At first nothing happened, but as he kept pushing, gradually the crack got bigger and bigger. One large piece of the shell fell away, and for the first time Valo was able to see the outside world. What a shock! He had imagined what the world might look like, but the reality was more than he could ever have dreamed. Above him was a huge bright blue sky and as he peeked through the gap, he could see grasslands and trees stretching away into the distance to the far horizon.

He continued to push against the shell and another large chunk fell away. Now there was enough room for him to squeeze out into the world beyond. Poking his nose out, the little dinosaur smelled the most fascinating smells and saw the most amazing sights. It was incredible, and the little dinosaur was overwhelmed. He had never imagined anything so wonderful. Squeezing through the gap he had made, he scrambled out onto the ground. Looking around he could see that he was on a narrow ledge that was only a few metres wide. Edging carefully forward, he peered over the edge and saw the valley far below him. He couldn't see how to get down, so looking to his right, he decided to follow the ledge and see where it led. Perhaps his parents were there in the valley below; he had to get down and try to find them. Very carefully, he stood up onto his legs. He had never tried to walk before and his legs felt very wobbly and shaky. As he took his first few steps, he fell over a couple of times, and it was hard to get his balance. After a few more tries, he started to use his strong tail to help him balance, and slowly he was able to make his way along the path. He turned around and took one final look at the shattered remains of the egg which had been the only home and security he had known, then he took a deep breath and started forward. Above him, he could hear the raptors still calling and arguing, and he stayed close to the wall of the path to stay out of sight.

Carefully, the little dinosaur made his way slowly along until he saw the path widen and turn downwards. Keeping in the shadows as much as he could, Valo continued to follow the path down and down towards the valley floor.

After a long walk, he arrived at the valley floor. The pterodactyls had gone and everything was very quiet. Looking around him, he couldn't tell what he should do or which way he should go. Perhaps he should call out to his parents and they would come and find him. Drawing a deep breath, he opened his mouth and tried to call them, but only a faint squeak came out. He tried again, and this time the squeak was a little louder. By the fourth attempt, he was able to make a much louder noise and he stopped to listen for his mother's gentle voice in reply. But here was nothing, just the wind blowing through the shrubs. He tried to call out again and again, but each time he waited there was no reply. Where were his parents? Where was anyone else?

Feeling very worried, he sat down and looked around. He had to try to decide the way forward, but the little chap had no idea where he was and no idea what to do. He felt so very tired and so he scrambled over to a large bush and crept into the middle to hide and try to sleep. All night long, the little dinosaur curled up into a tight ball on some leaves and slept. His dreams were filled with the egg flying through the air and then falling to the ground and his efforts to get out into the world beyond.

Hours later, the little dinosaur woke up and crawled out from under the bush. For the first time ever he felt hungry and thirsty. Inside his egg, everything he needed had been there for him, but now he would have to find something to eat and drink all by himself. Lifting up his head, he sniffed the air and could smell something interesting off to one side of his hideaway. Following the scent, Valo made his way carefully towards the source of the fascinating smell. He kept glancing up into the sky to make sure that the raptors had not returned, but there was no sign of them. Up ahead there was a small group of trees and as he approached them, he saw a clear stream of water flowing rapidly along the bank. Scrabbling down towards the edge, he bent down to drink. It was his first taste of water and it was wonderful. He looked up to check that there was no-one else around, and then lowered his head to take another long satisfying drink.

He felt better after his sleep and drink, but he still felt hungry but had no idea what to do about it. One thing was for certain, he had to find his parents.

Deciding that the best thing to do was to follow the stream, he set off along the bank. Every so often, he stopped and called out to his parents, but there was no reply. As the sun rose in the sky, he began to feel really hungry, and his tummy rumbled and gurgled. Looking around, he could see lots of plants and he wondered whether they might be good and tasty to eat. The first one he tried had a sweet taste and he munched happily on a few stems. The next one had bright yellow flowers which also tasted good and he was growing in confidence that he would be able to find nice things to eat. The next plant he tried however was not so successful. As he bit into the leaves, there was a horrid stinging sensation and he spat the large mouthful out onto the ground and shook his head. Yuk! Even though the leaves were gone, his mouth was still stinging, so he slipped down to the edge of the water and took a long drink to wash out his mouth and get rid of the taste and the stinging. When he climbed back up the bank, he made a note of the plant that had been so bad to eat and promised himself to be more careful in future.

All that day, the little dinosaur trudged along the banks of the stream, stopping to nibble on the various plants growing there, and still calling out, hoping that his parents would reply. Sadly, there was still no sign of either his parents, nor anyone else. Occasionally, he could see the pterodactyls flying a long way in the distance, but otherwise he was completely alone.

As the sun began to set in the sky, he looked for a safe place to spend his second night. Oh, how he missed the safety of his little egg. Up ahead was a large mass of prickly bushes and he carefully slid in under the low branches and once again curled into a ball to try to sleep. He was so very tired after all of the walking that he fell asleep straight away. He didn't hear any of the little night creatures who were scampering around the bank of the stream, or poked their little noses under the bush to see who was there.

The next morning, he slipped out of his hiding place and after a drink of water, continued his walk. Avoiding the stinging plants, and being careful when he tried something new, he had a good breakfast and started to walk more quickly as he got better at using his legs. Around mid-day, he decided to stop for a while to rest, and sat by the stream gazing out over the water to the world beyond. Suddenly, he heard a rustling and crunching noise behind him, and he jumped up and spun around in excitement.

"Mummy! Daddy!" he cried. There was no-one there! The little dinosaur scampered along the bank a short way and stopped to listen. The noise seemed to be coming from behind a bush. Surely now he was safe! Looking over the top of the bush, Valo couldn't see anyone, so he rushed around the side to greet his parents. It was doubly exciting as he had no idea what they looked like! Normally when a baby hatched from its egg, their parent was the very first one they saw, but for this little dinosaur, he had been all alone when he hatched up on the ledge, and so didn't know how his parents looked. However, that was not on his mind as be rushed around to greet them; he just knew that they would know each other.

As he rounded the bush he screeched to a halt. There was someone there, but not at all what he expected. Looking at him was a small dinosaur with a very long neck and a small head and ears. The dinosaur smiled at him and took a step towards him. He was shocked. Was this his mummy or Daddy? He gave a shy smile and asked "are you my Mummy or my daddy?". The other dinosaur looked very puzzled and then burst out laughing.

"No silly, I'm not your mummy or daddy. We're not even the same kind! What kind are YOU?"

"What do you mean" the little dinosaur replied "I don't know what kind of anything I am. I'm looking for my parents but I don't know where they are"

With that, a big fat tear fell from his eye. He suddenly felt very sad and alone.

"Hey don't cry" said the other dinosaur "My name is Philip. I can help you find your family. Where do you live?"

The little dinosaur shook his head "I don't know" he whispered "I was stolen from my parents before I hatched by two huge flyers. They dropped my egg with me inside it before reaching their nest and I landed on a ledge above the valley. When I climbed out of the egg, I was all alone and didn't know where to go. So, I just started walking along the river. Do you think you can help me get home?"

"We can try together," said Philip. "Do you know your name?"

The little dinosaur shook his head. "Other than the flyers I saw in the distance; you are the only one I've seen. You have a much longer neck than me, so I guess we are different kinds, but I just don't know!"

"Hmmm "mused Philip "I bet you don't really know what you look like either do you? Well, we can soon sort that out – follow me" With that, the Philip hurried off along the bank, with the little dinosaur close behind. Just around the bend in the stream, Philip stopped and turned back grinning. "Here we go".

The little dinosaur had no idea what he meant but the walked slowly towards a small pond of very still water and peered over. There, reflected in the water, was another dinosaur! He jumped back in fright – who was this? Were they friendly? Cautiously, he leant forward and looked down into the water again. When he blinked his eyes, the other dinosaur blinked his, when he nodded his head, the other dinosaur did the same. Suddenly he realised that he could see himself for the very first time! He had big blue eyes and beautiful shiny scales which reflected blues, reds and golds in the sunlight. He had a slim face and as he turned to one side, he could make out a lovely ruffle going across the top of his head and down his back. As he smiled at his reflection, he could see his beautiful white teeth smiling back at him.

Turning around to his new friend "Is that really ME?" he asked.

"It certainly is" Philip confirmed. "You can see that we are definitely not the same kind. I'm a Philomimus and if I'm not mistaken, you my friend are a Valoraptor. Yes, indeed I do believe that's what you are! I'm going to call you Valo!"

"Valo" breathed the little dinosaur, "my name is Valo and I'm a Valoraptor!"

Philip came over to Valo and laid his long neck gently over Valo's shoulder.

"So now that we know who you are, let's go and find your parents. Come on Valo let's go!"

The two friends began to walk alongside the stream which was growing larger and wider. They munched happily on the various plants growing on the bank, and Philip showed Valo which were the most yummy and which ones to avoid. Philip explained to Valo that his own parents had taught him all about which plants were safe to eat and which ones were dangerous.

Valo felt so much better to be with his new friend who seemed to know such a lot about everything. "This is so much nicer than being alone" he thought.

Around the middle of the day, they stopped and Philip decided he would like some fish for lunch. "Where can you get fish?" asked

Valo – "I've not seen any around here? Anyway, what's a fish?" Philip laughed, "Oh my, you do have a lot to learn – fish live in the water, and taste delicious. Come on, I'll show you what to do"

Philip slipped down the bank to the edge of the water, with Valo following close behind. As they stood peering into the water, Valo could see silvery shapes moving along under the surface. Some were really small, but now and again a very large one would glide past and disappear into the distance.

"Those, my friend, are fish" announced Philip and grinning at Valo he stepped very gently into the shallow water.

"Where are you going?" whispered Valo

"I'm going fishing" replies Philip "Just stay quiet and still and watch what I do".

Slowly and steadily, Philip went a little further into the water and then stood very still, watching and waiting. Very carefully, Philip lowered his head until it was just above the surface. Valo was watching absolutely fascinated – whatever was his friend going to do?

Quick as a flash, Philip dipped his head under the water and when he lifted his head up, he had a large fish in his mouth! Marching back up the bank, Philip proudly dropped his catch onto the floor and grinned at Valo. "Lunch is served" he said.

Valo looked uncertainly at the fish and then back at Philip. "Go on, tuck in" called Philip as he went back into the water "I'll be back in a moment"

Valo bent down and sniffed the fish. He was certainly hungry, and so he thought he would try this new food. He took a small nibble and YES it was delicious. In just two bites the fish was gone. How wonderful thought Valo.

Turning back towards the river, he saw Philip coming back towards him carrying his own fish which he ate in just one mouthful. "Excellent" said the little dinosaur, "Now it's your turn Valo"

"Me?" replied Valo uncertainly, "But I don't know how"

"Awww come on Valo, it's easy, I'll show you what to do"

Valo went carefully down into the water. He could feel the mud between his toes and the pull of the current as the water passed by. Looking down, he could only see some weeds waving under the water, but there were no fish. He looked back up to Philip "Just be patient" whispered his friend, "and keep looking"

Valo turned back and looked down into the water. Lowered his head as he has seen Philip do, he peered beneath the surface. Then he saw it! A large fish was coming straight towards him. This was his chance! Valo was so excited that he lunged forward to grab the fish, but he made such a splash that the fish swam away and poor Valo slipped found himself face down in the water!

Trying not to laugh, Philip encouraged his friend to try again. "Just take your time and be quiet" he repeated.

Valo shook the water from his eyes and lowered his head again to look down into the water. After a few moments, a fish appeared out of the gloom. Very slowly, just as he had seen his friend do, Valo dipped his head and grabbed the fish. He'd done it!

He scrambled up the bank towards Philip and grinning he dropped the huge fish on the floor.

"Well done Valo" said Philip "We'll make a fisher out of you yet!"

After lunch, they carried on walking, with Philip explaining all sorts of interesting things to Valo. He told him that the clouds carried rain water which would then fall from the sky and fill the streams and river, and that the big golden sun went to sleep every night just as they did. He told Valo how the night sun was there in case they needed light at night, but that it was not too bright so that those resting could easily get to sleep. Valo was amazed at how much his friend seemed to know.

Valo was fascinated by all the wonderful plants and shrubs surrounding them as they made their way along the bank. He scampered ahead of

Philip, sniffing at all the wonderful smells. A little way ahead, Valo could see a big area of brownish grey ground which was gleaming in the sunlight. He ran towards it to investigate. Philip was munching on a particularly delicious bunch of green shoots and didn't notice Valo disappear around the bend of the river.

Valo reached the shining surface and fascinated to feel the ground become squidgy between his toes. This wasn't water like the river. Whatever was it he wondered.

He walked slowly forward and the ground beneath him became more and more gooey. By now, Valo was up to his knees and he decided that this had not been such a good idea and that he should go back to find Philip. As he tried to turn around, the gooey mud in which he was standing seemed to grip onto his legs and he found it was almost impossible to move. He was stuck! Not only that, but he realised that he was slowly sinking!

Valo was really frightened and looked around for his friend, but Philip was no-where to be seen.

"Philip" shouted Valo, "Philip help me please. I'm stuck and I can't get out"

Valo looked all around but there was no sign of Philip.

"Philip – where are you – pleeeease!"

"Valo whatever is the matter" called Philip "Are you alright? I was just...."

Philip appeared around the corner and stopped in horror as he saw the little dinosaur stuck fast and sinking in the swampy mud.

"Hold on Valo – don't move" Philip shouted and turned and ran back along the bank.

"Philip don't leave me" cried Valo

Moments later, Philip came back to the edge of the swamp dragging a long branch in his teeth. Carefully he laid the branch down on the surface of the mud and gently pushed it towards Valo.

"Right Valo" he said "very carefully, take hold of the branch in your teeth and hold really tightly. Move very slowly and I will pull you out"

"Quickly Philip" shouted Valo, "I'm getting sucked in"

Valo turned and grabbed the branch between his teeth.

Philip did the same at his end of the branch, and began to gently pull the little dinosaur to safety.

Pull, pull, tug, tug, slowly, bit by bit, Philip pulled Valo back to the safety of the solid ground.

Finally, Valo lay face down on the grass and slowly turned to face Philip. Valo was covered on brown smelly goo.

"Oh Philip thank you – I might have been sucked all the way down if you hadn't been there". Valo was so relieved to be safe and a big tear rolled down his face and plopped onto the ground.

"Come on young Valo" replied Philip, "It's OK you're safe now. Let's go and get this goo washed off and you will feel much better. Just don't go wandering off on your own again Valo"

"Don't worry" his little friend replied "I promise I will stay with you from now on".

The two friends made their way to the edge of the water and managed to gently wash away all the yuky goo from the swamp. They climbed back up the bank and shook off the last droplets of water, and smiled at each other.

"That was a lucky escape Valo" said Philip seriously.

As they walked along, Valo noticed that Philip kept glancing around, as if looking for something or someone. Eventually, Valo asked him

"What's that matter Philip? What are you looking for? I told you that the ones you called pterodactyls that stole my egg are a long way behind us now. I think we should be safe"

"No" smiled Philip, "There's nothing to worry about. It's just that I know this area and I have some friends who live nearby and I was hoping we might see them. I would love you to meet them and say Hello".

"Are they your kind, or my kind" asked Valo

Philip laughed. "Neither my friend. Let's wait and see shall we."

Valo felt very excited at the idea of meeting new friends. He hoped that they might know his parents and help him to find them. He kept looking left and right to try to see if Philip's friends were close by, but so far, he saw and heard nothing.

Late into the afternoon, they stopped by some wonderful tasty bushes and had their meal. These were new plants that Valo had never seen before and he was really enjoying them, together with some sweet blue berries growing nearby. He decided it was so much nicer to share meals with a friend, rather than eating on his own. In fact, everything had seemed better since he met Philip. He just wished he knew where they were going and how he would ever find his mummy and daddy.

He looked up from munching on the berry bush and saw that Philip was staring with a huge grin on his face across the open space behind him. Spinning around Valo saw two small dinosaurs walking towards them. Philip was right, neither of them were his kind.

The smaller of the two dinosaurs was about the same height as Valo, but where Valo was slim and walked on his two hind feet, this dinosaur walked on all four feet and has a huge crest behind their head and three long horns above their face. This dinosaur had huge brown eyes and beautiful gold and bronze stripes alone each side of their body. The second dinosaur was a little taller but still walked on all four feet. Instead of the crest and horns, this one has a huge long spike protruding directly out from their head. This time, the dinosaur that blue eyes, and zigzag markings of green and blue.

Valo gazed in amazement; how many different kinds could there be?

Philip stepped forward – "Valo my friend, these are the ones I was telling you about. Valo, please meet Rhianne, she's a Rhiannotop, and Lola, who as you can see is a Lolasaurophus, two of my very special friends" Valo shyly walked forwards and the three dinosaurs rubbed noses in greeting.

"Do you know my mummy and daddy?" blurted out Valo.

"Your mummy and daddy?" asked the Lolasaurophus, "No I don't sorry. What kind are you Valo? I haven't seen your kind here before."

Valo's heart sunk. He was so sure that these new friends would be able to help him find his parents, but he was just as lost as before.

Gulping back his tears, Valo turned to the two new dinosaurs. "I'm called Valo" he said "I'm a Valoraptor. Philip is trying to help me find my mummy and daddy, but we don't know where they are"

"Well, we can help too" said the Rhiannotop. "When did you last see your parents?"

"I've never seen them" sniffed Valo, and he explained how the pterodactyls had taken his egg from the nest and how he had hatched all alone on the ledge. He told them how Philip had found him and how he was trying to find his way home.

"Let's start at the beginning" said Philip "Can you tell us anything at all that you remember, however small. It might just give us a clue"

The four little dinosaurs sat down and Valo closed his eyes, trying to remember.

"When I was in my egg, I remember I felt warm and safe. I was never hungry or thirsty and everything was dark and snug. Sometimes, I could hear my mummy and daddy and I remember my mummy singing to me" As Valo spoke, a large tear ran slowly down his face and splashed on the ground.

"What about smells?" asked Lola. "Smells are usually really helpful"

Valo thought for a moment. "That's difficult" he said, "I'm still learning what everything is. Yesterday morning, Philip and I had some lovely minty leaves to eat, and the smell did seem familiar. I think I remember it, but I'm just not sure."

"That's good Valo" encouraged Philip "Yes that was a lucky find. Minty leaves are really unusual so if we find some more that might give us a clue. What about anything else?"

Valo thought for a moment and then sadly shook his head. "Never mind" said Rhianne, "I'm sure we'll find your parents. We can do it together!"

"Come on everyone" called Philip, "let's get going. It's time to find Valo's mummy and daddy"

The four little dinosaurs moved off, still following the river. The small stream had become wider and deeper, but they could still easily see the opposite bank.

As the big golden sun started to sink in the sky, the four friends decided it would soon be time for them to sleep too. Valo found a warm hollow in a group of trees and they all snuggled down together to rest. It was so good to have others to cuddle down with, and for the first time, Valo began to feel safe and hopeful that they really would find his parents.

Closing his eyes, he began to think about his mummy and daddy and a small smile played on his lips as he drifted off to sleep.

"Valo, Valo where are you? I can't find you!"

Valo work with a start. Who was calling him? The voice sounded just like his mummy! Looking around, he saw that the others were all curled up fast sleep. Sadly, he realised that he must have been dreaming. Lifting up his head, he peered over the edge of the hollow but he couldn't see anyone. Although the night sun was there in the sky, it was only very small and slim and was not sharing very much light. Valo waited and listened, but he could only hear the wind gently blowing in the nearby trees. Sighing, he lay back down again and closed his eyes.

The next morning, the big golden sun was hidden behind clouds and the day felt cold and damp. Valo stood up and shivered. He decided he was hungry and so crept out of the hollow so as not to wake the others, and made his way over to some interesting looking bushes. To his delight, he found some juicy red berries and he began to tuck in, enjoying the sweet juice that ran down his chin.

"Hey, leave some for us!" called a familiar voice. Spinning round, Valo saw the others approaching "Come on" he said, "there's plenty for everyone!"

They all tucked in with Gusto, and after a wonderful breakfast of berries and delicious tasty leaves, they had a long drink at the river and once again began to walk.

"There are four of us" mused Valo "and each of us is a different kind. Just how many kinds ARE there?"

"That's a hard question" replied Philip, "No-one really knows. Some kinds look very much alike, but others look very different. Some can fly, like the pterodactyls that stole your egg, and others are swimmers"

"What's a swimmer?"

Lola laughed "Gosh Valo, you really do have a lot to learn! Swimmers go into the water. Some live there all the time, like fish, but others just swim for fun or to cross the water to the other side"

"Are you all swimmers?" asked Valo.

Philip laughed, "No we aren't all swimmers. I can swim a little bit but I'd rather just paddle in the shallow water or be on dry land. What about you Lola and Rhianne, are you swimmers?"

"Yes Yes! "they squealed "We love swimming. We can use our tails to help us and it's great fun. Just remember Valo, you NEVER go too far from the bank. That can be dangerous."

Valo looked confused "what do you mean dangerous?" he asked

"Well sometimes the water can go very fast and it might carry you away" explained Lola

"And there are other kinds who live in the water who are dangerous too. They don't like it when other kinds are in the water and they are big and scary. I wouldn't want to get too close to them"

"Me neither" said Rhianne with a shudder.

Valo was amazed and how much the others knew about the world around them. He was very grateful that they were travelling with him.

The further along the river bank they walked, the wider the river grew. By the time the stopped for lunch they could only just see the other side. The four friends were stunned at how big the small stream had grown. They had been grazing all morning and so apart from a quick paddle and drink, they didn't stop for lunch. Up ahead, they could see some very tall hills with Philip told them were really mountains. There was a lot of vegetation growing on the bottom slopes and there were white tops which glistened in the sunlight. They looked huge and Valo wondered if there might be someone there who knew his parents.

Around a bend in the river, the most amazing sight greeted them. The river had opened into a large lake with reed banks along the edge. It was the biggest area of water that any of them had ever seen, and they stood gazing in wonder at this new discovery. There was a tiny island in the middle of the lake, but other than that there was nothing to be seen.

Late that afternoon, they decided to sit and rest for a while. Valo's feet were a bit sore from walking so far and everyone felt tired. They were all sitting looking across the water lost in thought when Philip suddenly sat bolt upright.

"SHHH – did you hear that" he whispered

"What?" replied Valo

"That noise – can't you hear it? It sounds like someone or something is coming this way!"

"Perhaps it's my mummy and daddy" shouted Valo "Mummy, Daddy, it's me – I'm over here!"

"Be quiet please Valo" hissed Lola – "we need to wait and see who it is"

Valo was torn between listening to his friends and running to see his parents.

Rhianne pulled Valo into the tall grass where the others were hiding. "Just wait and see Valo, we don't know this area and we don't know who lives here. We need to be quiet and stay out of sight until we are sure it's safe".

"But I'm sure it must be my...."

"Hush Valo! Don't make a sound" ordered Philip.

Peering through the grass to the plain beyond, the four waited, listening carefully. Who was it? Were they friends, or was there danger?

Valo's heart was beating fast with a mixture of excitement and concern.

As they waited quietly, they could hear branches rustling and the crunching of leaves underfoot. The ground underneath them trembled at little and a really nasty smell came towards them on the breeze. Whatever was it?

Then from behind some huge trees came the most enormous dinosaur that they had ever seen. Taller than the surrounding trees, the huge creature was a green / brown colour with a huge head and very small front arms. Slowly it walked towards the lake, and they could see it had massive feet with great big sharp curved claws and a wide sweeping tail which it held up in the air. By far the most frightening thing was the creature's huge mouth and rows of sharp pointed teeth. As it approached their hiding place, it stopped, and sniffed the air, looking around.

"It can smell us" whispered Philip "Stay absolutely quiet and still whatever happens".

Valo was shaking with fright. He had never imagined such a thing could exist. He had a hundred questions, but obeyed Philip and kept absolutely still.

The enormous dinosaur continued to look around and sniff, and then finally opened his mouth and roared! The sound made the ground around them tremble, and was the most terrifying sound that they had ever heard. Their instinct was to run, but Philip had told them to stay and they trusted their friend.

The dinosaur moved slowly towards the stand of grass where they were crouching and once again sniffed the air. Then he leant forward and roared. His breath blew the grass away, and the four friends could be seen crouching together.

"RUUUN" screamed Philip "quick into the water & swim."

Valo, Rhianne, Lola and Philip turned and scrambled down the bank into the water and began to swim away from the bank and towards the little island in the middle of the lake. The water very quickly became too deep to walk and Valo, who had never tried to swim before, kept slipping under the water. Lola and Rhianne were swimming well, and Philip was using is long neck to keep his head above the water. Valo however was in trouble. His small front arms just didn't have the strength to swim and his heavy tail and back legs were pulling him down under the surface. Philip could see his young friend was struggling and, ducking his head under the water, he caught his long neck underneath Valo to bring him to the surface and support him.

Valo came out of the water coughing and spluttering and took a great gasp of air.

"We'll be OK Valo" gasped Philip "I've got you".

Meanwhile the huge dinosaur had plunged into the water after them. Like Valo, his front arms were small, but he was so tall that at first there was no need for him to swim and he strode steadily into the water, roaring his anger. As the water became deeper, he was no longer able to walk and not being a swimmer, he was forced to stop. Staring at the four little ones making their way to the island, he roared in frustration one final time and turned back to the bank.

Reaching the island, the four little friends scrambled up the muddy bank and looked back across the water.

"I think we'll be safe here," said Lola

"Do you think he saw us?" asked Valo

"Yes, but he can't get to us" replied Rhianne "Whatever is it?"

"That is not the kind you want to meet very often," said Philip. "That is a King Dinosaur, a Tyrannosaurus Rex. I've only ever heard about them and never seen one before. I wasn't even sure that they were real."

Valo was still shaking. He had never been so scared, even when his egg had been stolen by the pterodactyls. He had never tried to swim before and was pretty sure he never wanted to swim again.

Looking back across the water, they could see the Rex striding back and disappear down a slope and into the cover of the trees.

Valo gave a small smile turned to Lola "Well you were right Lola, that was definitely not my mummy and daddy!"

Rhianne addressed the small group "I'm sorry everyone" she said, "but we have to swim again!"

"Oh no thank you" said Valo, "I don't think a Valoraptor is meant to be a swimmer"

"Maybe not" she replied, "But we are on an island Valo, we need to swim to get to the other side"

Valo's heart sank. Looking at the opposite bank, it really did look a very long way away.

"Come on young Valo, you can do it" encouraged Philip. "Let's all swim together"

In a long line, they all stood up and walked across the tiny rocky island and stepped down once again into the water.

"Why don't you try to swim on your back and use your tail and strong back legs" suggested Lola.

"Great idea" said Rhianne" That way you won't get water up your nose. Come on Valo, let's give it a try."

"Come on "said Lola, "I'll swim right beside you".

Valo turned around and carefully lowered himself onto his back and started to kick his legs and waggle his tail. This really was much easier! He looked to the side and saw Lola swimming next to him, with Rhianne swimming next to her. Above him, he could see that the big golden sun was almost gone and the night sun could be seen peeping from behind a cloud.

By the time they arrived on the opposite bank, the four little dinosaurs were exhausted. They climbed up the slope and fell down in a tangled heap together and were asleep straight away.

The next morning the four travellers woke up and cautiously looked to see if there was any sign of the Rex. "I think it's gone "said a very relieved Valo "I never saw anything so big. Thank you everyone for helping me in the water. I would never had made it if it wasn't for you"

"You're welcome" smiled Lola. "I'm hungry. Let's go and find something to eat"

As she stood up, she saw four large fish, a large pile of juicy fresh berries and another pile of leaves and grasses right beside their sleeping place.

"Wow! Come and look at this. Breakfast! However did this get here?

As they were munching on their delicious but unexpected breakfast, they kept a look out to see if anyone was about.

Philip had really good hearing, and he kept stopping to lift his head and look around. He was sure he could hear something, but he wasn't sure what it could be.

"There it is again" he whispered.

"Is it the Rex!?" Valo replied looking scared.

"No, it sounds like someone giggling!"

"Giggling? Are you certain?

"Yes, it's coming from over there. I'm going to see what it is".

"Be careful" warned Rhianne

Philip started to walk towards a group of bushes. Yes, there it was again, a small high giggle. Philip was quite a tall dinosaur, and as he reached the bushes, he was able to look down into the middle. There, crouched together, were two small dinosaurs!

Lowering his head, he peered down at them.

"Well hello "he said "Who are you two?"

The smallest dinosaur giggled again "Hello! I'm Jaredadon and this is my sister Jacie. Did you like your breakfast?"

Philip was joined by Lola Rhianne and Valo. "Did YOU bring our breakfast?" Valo asked. "That was so very kind of you".

"Yes we did, oh yes indeed "replied Jacie, "we saw you swimming across the lake away from that Rex. We were very scared for you and watched where you made your den so we could bring you something to eat this morning."

Philip looked down at the two small dinosaurs. "Thank you very much for your kindness. Please, come and join us. My name is Philip, and these are my friends Valo, Rhianne and Lola"

Valo couldn't wait any longer.

"Please" he said, "have you seen my mummy and daddy?"

Jared and Jacie looked up at Valo "I don't think so" said Jaden, "What do your parents look like?"

Poor Valo sadly shook his head and explained that he had never seen his parents, but they were all on their way to find them.

"I expect they look a lot like Valo" said Philip wisely. "He's a Valoraptor you know".

"Gosh, I've never heard of one of that kind" said Jacie, "but come to look at you, you are a little bit familiar".

That was the first good news Valo had had. If Jacie and Jared recognised his kind, then perhaps his mummy and daddy might be nearby.

After breakfast, the little group started walking again. This side of the river seemed very different. There were not so many trees, and there were large areas where the ground was stony and dusty. Plants grew along the bank, so there was plenty of food, and at lunchtime they caught some fish which they shared together.

As the big golden sun was high in the sky, the little group were making their way past a tall rocky ridge when they heard a deep rumbling sound and a few stones and some soil trickled down the side of the ridge.

"It's the Rex!" screamed Lola "Quick – hide!"

"No it's OK "Jared called, "It's a shaking. Haven't you felt one before?"

"No never" replied Lola

"What's a shaki…"

Before Valo could finish speaking the rumbling noise came again, but this time much louder. The friends were finding it difficult to stand in the same place as the ground underneath them seemed to move and roll just like the water on the lake.

"Stay close together" shouted Philip. "Stand with your legs apart it will be easier to keep steady"

"That's easy for you to say" said Valo," I only have two legs to stand on not four!"

The shaking was getting stronger and stronger and the friends all clung together, supporting one another. Valo squeezed his eyes tightly shut. The rumblings were getting louder and then there was a huge crash and thud as a huge lump of rock fell from the rock face above, narrowly missing the little group. Then, almost as quickly as it began, the shaking stopped and everything was quiet. Valo opened his eyes to look around.

They were all safe, although they were covered in dirt and dust.

"Oh my" breathed Lola "What was that?"

"It's called a shaking" explained Jared, "It happens sometimes but that was a pretty big one. Is everyone OK?"

"An old dinosaur who lived nearby used to tell us about this. He was a Thesaurus, and he knew everything about everything. I've never seen one before though", said Philip.

Valo shook himself, "Come on everyone, let's keep moving."

The big rock that had fallen had blocked their path along the river, and so they turned inland, still making their way towards the mountains in the distance. Scrambling down a slope, decided it would be fun to have a race to the next tree. Jared and Jacie were the smallest so they were given a head start.

"One, two three GO!" shouted Philip, and the dinosaurs all ran as fast as they could. Valo was a very fast runner, but Philip and Lola and Rhianne were right behind him. Running as fast as he could, he managed to overtake Jacie and Jared and as he neared the trees he gasped in horror! The ground had disappeared! A huge gap in the earth had opened up which stretched as far as he could see to the left and the right. He spun run and shouted "STOP!" as loudly as he could as the others raced towards him. The others immediately slowed down and gathered round Valo and the edge of the cleft. The crevasse was wider than Valo was tall and as they peered down, they couldn't see the bottom.

"Gosh that was close" breathed Jacie, "what are we going to do?"

"I don't think I can jump over" said Philip, "it's just too far. Should we walk along the edge and see how far the gap goes?"

"We can go and see" offered Jared, "Come on Jacie, let's go and see what we can find."

The two little dinosaurs scampered off while the others sat down to wait.

"Does anyone know what caused this?" asked Philip, "I wonder if it is anything to do with the shaking."

"I think it must be" replied Lola, "the ground was shaking so much I wouldn't be surprised".

After a little while, Jacie and Jared came running back to the group. "There's a huge gap that goes a long long way and just seems to get bigger. If we're going to get across, I think this is the best place to try." said Lola.

"I don't think we can try to jump over" said Philip, "I certainly couldn't manage it. Does anyone have any ideas?"

"What we need is a bridge" suggested Rhianne, "a way to walk across the gap."

"That's a really good idea Rhianne, but how can we find a bridge?"

"Why don't we try to make one?" suggested Valo.

"But how could we do that?" asked Lola, "I've never done anything like that before."

"We need something strong to go across the gap" said Valo. "Let's all put our heads together; there must be a way we can do this."

"Do you think we could climb down and then up the other side?" suggested Lola.

"No, Lola, it's a good idea" replied Philip, "but I don't think we could. It's so steep that I wouldn't be able to climb down and definitely I wouldn't be able to climb back up the other side. I can't even see the bottom."

"Hey – Hello – Can you hear us? Can you see us? We're over here!"

The friends all looked up, and to their astonishment they could see two new dinosaurs standing on the other side of the gap, waving at them.

"Hello!" shouted Valo – "Who are you?"

"I'm Danny, I'm a Dannymimus"

"And I'm Summer" said the other dinosaur "I'm a Summersaurus. Who are you? Are you stuck?"

"We're trying to find my mummy and Daddy" called Valo. "Please, do you know my parents?"

"I don't know" said Summer "What kind are you, and where do your parents live?"

"I don't know" replied Valo, "My name is Valo, and I'm a Valoraptor. We are trying to find my mummy and daddy, and we've walked such a long way. We were on the other side of the river but we had to swim across to escape a huge dinosaur."

"It was a Rex" said Rhianne, "he was chasing us so we had to swim to the island, and then swim right across to this side, and then we met Jacie and Jared here.

"Goodness what a scary adventure you've all had" responded Summer, "Are you trying to get across the big gap? It's certainly a big one. It wasn't here yesterday so it must have happened with the shaking".

"Yes" replied Philip, "We're trying to work out how to do it but we're stuck! It's too far to jump over and we can't get down either. Jacie and Jared went to look and the gap goes on a long way so I don't think we can get around it either."

"I think we need a bridge" said Rhianne, "but we don't know where we could find one."

"I think you should make a bridge" suggested Danny.

"MAKE one?" asked Philip, "but how?"

"See that tree over there" pointed Danny, "that might work"

"What do you mean" asked Rhianne, "we can't climb up a tree, and even if we could, that wouldn't get us across the gap."

They all looked towards the tall tree which was growing not far from the edge of the big gap. It was quite a wide strong looking tree, with strong branches at the top.

Valo shook his head. He agreed with Rhianne. He didn't see how the tree could help them get across to the other side.

"You need to push it" shouted Summer "Push the tree over to us!"

"That's right" called Danny "Summer is right, push the tree over to us!"

"What do you mean?" asked Philip, "the tree is on this side, how could we get it over to you?"

Suddenly Valo started to jump up and down with excitement "I can see it" he cried "I know what you mean! If we push the tree and it falls over the gap, we can carefully walk across the tree like a bridge to the other side! I really think it might work!"

"Do you really think we could?" asked Jacie "It's a very tall tree, but if we can do it, I think it might work!"

Lola and Rhianne looked at one another "This is a job for us" they said. "We are really strong, although we are not very big. I think if we all push together, we can push the tree over the gap! Valo, you have really strong front claws. Do you think you can dig around the bottom of the tree to get some of the soil away? Then if we all push together, I think we can push the tree over."

Valo stepped forward, "Let's try" he said, and he bent over and began to dig as fast as he could around the base of the tree.

It was very hard work, but Valo was the only one with claws that could dig well enough. Valo's front legs were quite short so it meant that he had to get his head right down to the ground to dig. The other dinosaurs were watching and encouraging their friend. Valo worked really hard at digging, and gradually, a large hole began to appear around the base of the tree trunk.

"Keep going Valo" called Danny"

"You can do it" encouraged Summer

Valo lifted up his head from the hole. He was covered in soil, but he was determined to dig as far as he could. He knew it was the only way to get across the gap and find his mummy and daddy.

After a long time and a lot of digging, Valo clambered out of the large hole he had dug. The roots of the tree could clearly be seen at the bottom.

"Right," shouted Danny "everyone must get together and push as hard as you can. Keep on pushing and the tree should fall across the gap."

"Come on everyone" cried Valo "let's all get together and push. Be careful not to get close to the edge. Ready, Steady PUUUUUSH!"

Philip, Valo and Rhianne and Lola all pushed on the tree as hard as they could. Jacie and Jared were really too small to help, but were jumping up and down and calling out to encourage them.

At first nothing happened. "Perhaps you need to dig some more" ventured Lola.

"Let's try again" replied Valo, "One Two THREEEEE PUUUUSH!"

"There" cried Philip, "I felt it move!"

"Yes, it did – come on everyone -HEEEEAAAAVE!"

The four friends pushed as hard as they could. Yes! The tree was moving!

"Keep going! I can see it moving" yelled Summer.

Suddenly, there was a loud groaning and cracking sound, and the trunk of the tree began to sway.

"Look out!" cried Philip "it's going to fall!"

The huge tree began to creak and sway, and then with an awful crashing sound, it fell across the gap, with the top landing on the other side of the gap. They had done it!

A great cheer went up from the creatures on both sides of the gap! A thick cloud of dust rose up, and as it cleared, they could see Summer and Danny on the other side, jumping up and down and cheering!

"Well done well done!" they shouted. "Come on everyone, over you come!"

"I think the small ones should go first" said Philip. "Come on Jacie and Jared, show us how it's done!"

The two smallest dinosaurs stepped nervously and carefully onto the fallen tree trunk.

"Just take care and don't look down. Keep your eyes on Summer and Danny and go slowly."

Jacie and Jared began to walk slowly across the gap. The tree was quite wide and they were very grateful that it wasn't wobbly!

"Keep going!" encouraged Summer," you're nearly there"

Edging further and further, the two adventurers scrambled to the edge of the fallen trunk and jumped down onto the other side.

"Well done!" said Danny "Right – who's next?"

The four remaining friends looked fearfully at each other.

"Righto, I guess this is up to me" said Valo, and he stepped forward and up onto the fallen tree. Valo was a lot bigger than Jace and Jared and he had to walk very carefully, putting one foot very slowly in front of the other. He began to feel quite confident and looked back at Philip and the others. "Look at me" he called, "it's not too bad at…" With that, Valo felt his foot slip from under him, and he fell forward onto the fallen tree. Lola screamed in fright and everyone held their breath.

Valo managed to dig his claws into the bark and very very gradually he pulled his foot back up onto the tree and started to edge his way forward again. It was a little wobbly, but Valo kept going and he made his way across without any more problems.

"Come on" he shouted over to the others "next one!"

Rhianne and Lola made their way one by one, and they too got over without any mishaps.

Finally, it was Philip's turn. He took a deep breath and looked down. It did seem a very long way.

"Don't look down!" shouted Valo, "keep looking at me – you'll be fine".

Philip stepped up onto the log and, using his tail to help him balance, he carefully started forward. Philip felt the log sway a little and he tried to dig his toes into the wood to keep a good grip.

"Keep going" called Valo "come on my friend you can do it."

Philip had reached the middle of the tree trunk, and stopped for a moment. He was starting to feel that it really would be OK. He lifted his foot up to take the next step when there was a horrid cracking sound. Turning his head around, Philip could see that the tree was starting to sag and right behind him there was a loud sound of the splintering of wood. The tree was breaking up!

Philip looked back at his friends on the side in front of him.

"Quick, quick – come on Philip – COME ON!" called Valo, his voice trembling

Philip took a deep breath and started walking again. The tree started to dip and sway under his weight as he scrambled towards the end.

"Come on Philip – JUUUMP!" screamed Valo

With a final effort, Philip rushed forward and flung himself off the end of the tree and onto safe ground. He'd made it!

He looked back as the tree finally snapped and the two halves fell tumbling and twisting down into the gap.

The others rushed forward to greet Philip. They were all so relieved to have made it safely across.

"Danny, Summer thank you. If it wasn't for your idea, we would still be stuck on the other side" whispered Valo.

"Well Valo, let's look at you." said Summer coming up beside him. "Valoraptor you said? I must say, you do look quite familiar."

"Oh really!" cried Valo, "Do you know my mummy and daddy? Do you know where they are? I so want to find them."

"Well,", replied Summer, "I'm not sure, but come with me, I think I know someone who can help." She turned to walk up the slope away from the gap, and the other travellers followed behind.

"Where do you think we're going?" asked Valo

"I don't know" responded Philip, "Let's just wait and see".

Trudging up to the top of the rise, they could see the stream they had been following off to their right. Suddenly Valo stopped. There was a large patch of minty plants growing next to a bush of ripe red berries. "Look Philip" he called, "minty plants, just like the ones we had when we first met – remember I said that the smell seemed familiar?"

The little group made their way down to the water's edge and along the bank. They stopped for a long drink of the clear refreshing water. Valo walked carefully into the shallows to wash the dust off and as he walked back up onto the bank, he could see his friends tucking into some sweet grass and berries.

"What a lucky Valoraptor I am" he thought, "I would never have come this far without my friends."

"Where are we going Summer" asked Valo as he munched on some juicy berries.

"We're going to see a friend of mine" she replied with a gentle smile, "I have a feeling that they will be able to help us find your mummy and daddy."

Valo felt so excited, and was anxious to get going, but he knew everyone needed to eat and rest after their dangerous crossing on the tree bridge.

After they had all finished eating, Danny announced it was time to go. The eight little friends started to walk along the river bank. Valo kept stopping to smell and sniff the air. There was something familiar about this place, but he didn't know what it could be. He tried to remember whether it was something from when he was in his egg, but he just didn't know.

Just up ahead, Valo saw Summer stop and then turn off the path. "This way" she called. Summer made her way along the track until they came to a large tree under which sat a very large but friendly looking dinosaur.

"This is my friend" Summer announced "He is a very wise dinosaur, and he knows everything that has ever happened here. His job is to keep the memories. He's a very special kind – a Memodon".

Valo stepped forward "I'm so pleased to meet you" he said "My name is Valo and I'm…"

"Yes I know", interrupted the Memodon, "you're a Valoraptor."

"Yes I am" cried Valo "how did you know.? Please, can you help me, I'm looking for my parents, do you know them?"

"Well" said the Memodon kindly " I remember that two dinosaurs who look very much like you had their egg stolen by pterodactyls. They were very sad and have been looking everywhere to try to find their egg. Some of us have joined in the search along the riverbank, but we have not been able to find any sign of their egg or their baby"

"That's ME" cried Valo. "I'm the Valoraptor that was in the stolen egg. I met my friends and they have been helping me to look for my mummy and daddy. Please, can you help me?"

"Come with me" said the Memodon as he stood up and started back towards the river.

Valo followed closely behind. Did this dinosaur really know his parents? He felt so excited; was this finally the end of his search?

The little party made their way around a stand of trees, and Valo could see two large dinosaurs standing by a berry bush. They were standing on their strong back legs and had Valo could see their beautiful red blue and gold colours reflected in the sunlight, and the beautiful frill flowing down their backs. The same colours that he had seen when he had looked at his own reflection in the water when he first met Philip.

Was it? Could it be?

Valo couldn't hold back any longer. He rushed towards them shouting "MUMMY, DADDY it's me, it's Valo!"

The two dinosaurs turned at the sound of his voice.

"My darling baby! Can it really be you? "They rushed towards each other and were jumping up and down with happiness.

"Oh mummy, daddy, I can't believe I found you. I would never have managed it if it wasn't for my friends here. I've had such an adventure!"

61

"We looked everywhere for your egg" said his daddy, "but there was no clue as to where the pterodactyls had taken you. We all looked and looked, but no-one knew where you were."

"But you're home now" said Valo's mummy with tears in her eyes.

The Memodon smiled "this will make quite a story young Valo. I think we should all sit down, and you and your friends can tell us all about it"

And that's exactly what they did.

Lightning Source UK Ltd.
Milton Keynes UK
UKHW050710121221
395442UK00005B/87